Library of Congress Cataloging in Publication Data
Vincent, Gabrielle.
Merry Christmas, Ernest and Celestine.
Translation of: Noël chez Ernest et Célestine.
Summary: Even though they have no money, Ernest
and Celestine use their ingenuity to make a Christmas
party for their friends, knowing that it is love and
friendship and not money that really matters.
[1. Christmas—Fiction. 2. Bears—Fiction. 3. Mice—Fiction]
I. Title   PZ7.V744Me 1984   [E]   83-14155
ISBN 0-688-02605-2   ISBN 0-688-02606-0 (lib. bdg.)

GABRIELLE VINCENT

Merry Christmas, Ernest and Celestine

GREENWILLOW BOOKS
New York

"It's almost Christmas, Ernest.
You promised we could have a party. Remember?"

"But we don't have any
money, Celestine."

"We don't need money
for a party, Ernest."

"What about the tree
and the decorations
and the presents
and the cake?"

"Oh, Ernest, I know we can do it!"
"It's too cold to think about parties, Celestine. Come on."

"We can get
a tree in
the woods."

"You can play
the violin.
We can play
games and sing."

"But, Celestine,
what will
we eat?"

"You can make a cake
and we can have
orange juice
and cocoa.

And we can make
the presents

and the
decorations."

"Say yes, Ernest! Say yes!"

"I'm sorry Celestine. Not this year."
"But you promised, Ernest."

"You're right, Celestine. I *did*
promise. We'll have a party."

"Oh, Ernest, isn't this fun?"

"See, Ernest,
I told you
you could draw."

"I'm almost finished with the presents, Ernest.
   Come and look."
"I'm taking the cake out of the oven, Celestine.
   I'll be there in a minute."

"Look, Ernest, there are all sorts of things we can use."

"Not bad!

And a perfect dress
for Celestine!"

"Write neatly, Celestine, and
    don't forget to invite Cousin Max."
"Oh, Ernest, he's too old. He'll
    spoil the party."
"Don't be silly, Celestine. And
    hurry up. We have a lot to do."

"So where's the great Christmas party?"

"... and this is for you ..."

"You call that a Christmas tree?"

"Some baby must have
made the decorations."

"Don't listen to him, Celestine.
It's a beautiful tree!"

"Ernest, come quickly. Santa Claus is here.

Ernest?

Where are you, Ernest?

I can't find Ernest."

"Celestine,
now do you
recognize me?"

"More, more.
Bravo, Ernest and Celestine!"

"A story, Ernest. Tell us a story."

"Once upon a time, in a distant country . . ."

"Look! It's time to go home already."

"Thank you, Ernest.
I had a wonderful
time."

"I'm sorry I was mean,
Celestine.
It was a
splendid party.
May I come again
next year?"

"We did it, Ernest! We did it!

And we WILL have another
party next year!

Merry Christmas, Ernest."

"Merry Christmas, Celestine."